MAGICAL
TALES

PaRragon

Bath · New York · Cologne · Melbourne · Delhi
Hong Kong · Shenzhen · Singapore

Contents

Merry's Big Wish

Once upon a time there was a beautiful wooden horse named Merry who lived on a merry-go-round on the end of a seaside pier. But Merry wasn't just an ordinary wooden horse. He was very special! Every day people would come along to pat his nose and make a wish. And

almost always that wish would come true. For you see, Merry was said to have come from a magical land far away.

Merry loved giving rides to all the little children, and he loved making wishes come true. But Merry had a wish of his own. He wished he were real, so that he could gallop across the soft sand and splash through gentle waves on the seashore.

One night, when everyone had gone home for the day, Merry heard a neigh and a beautiful white mare appeared.

"Come with me," called the mare.

"I can't," replied Merry. "I'm not real."

"Anything is possible," said the mare, blowing softly on Merry's well-rubbed nose.

Suddenly a strange feeling came over Merry. His nose began to tingle and his legs began to twitch. Then he kicked his legs into the air and he was free. He raced after the white mare and splashed through the waves.

"Neigghhh!" cried Merry, as he and the white mare galloped on and on through the night. They didn't stop until they came to a faraway land full of snowy white horses.

"Where are we?" asked Merry.

"This is your home," replied the white mare. "The land where you came from. And all these horses are your brothers and sisters. From now on you will live here with us."

"But what about the merry-go-round and all the little children? And what about the wishes?"

"Don't worry," replied the white mare. "You can work on the merry-go-round each day, then return home each night."

"Neigghhh!" squealed Merry, tossing his mane into the air. "Now I am the happiest horse in the world."

Jack and the Beanstalk

Once upon a time there was a boy called Jack. He lived with his mother in a cottage. They were very poor.

One day, Jack's mother said, "We have no food left to eat and no money to buy it with. Take the cow to market and sell her."

So Jack took the cow to market. On the way, Jack met a very old man walking along the road.

"Where are you going?" asked the old man.

"I am going to market to sell the cow," said Jack. The old man offered Jack five magic beans for the cow. Jack agreed and sold the cow, then took the beans home.

"I sold the cow for five magic beans," he told his mother.

"Five beans!" she said. She was cross! She threw the magic beans out of the window.

Then she sent Jack to bed without any supper.

In the morning, Jack woke up. He looked out of the window. There was a giant beanstalk. It went up, up into the sky.

Jack climbed up the beanstalk.

At the top, there was a giant castle. Jack knocked on the door. The door opened.

Jack went in. Everything in the castle was enormous. That was because a giant and his wife lived in the castle.

"Fee, fi, fo, fum!" said the giant. "I want my breakfast."
Jack was afraid.

"You must hide," said the giant's wife, "or my husband will
eat you."

Jack hid from the giant.

The giant sat down at the table. Then he
put a hen on the table.

"Hen, lay an egg!" said the giant. The
hen laid a golden egg.

"Here is your breakfast," said the
giant's wife.

His wife gave him a very big breakfast.

The giant ate his breakfast. Then he felt
very sleepy. "Time for my nap," he said.

Soon he was fast asleep.

"A golden egg!" said Jack. "I will take the hen.
She will lay golden eggs and make us rich."

"Cluck!" said the hen. The giant woke up! Jack
ran to the beanstalk. The giant ran after him.

But Jack got his axe and chopped down
the beanstalk.

When the beanstalk fell to the ground,
the giant came crashing down with it.
That was the end of him!

Then the hen laid a golden egg.

And soon Jack and his mother weren't poor
any more!

The Powerful Spell

The sky went black and the villagers ran for their lives. "Help! Help!" they cried, as they dashed for the safety of the castle. "The dragon is back!"

Hovering above the thick stone castle walls, its giant, red, scaly wings outstretched, was a huge and terrible dragon.

"Curses!" snarled the dragon, blasting the castle with fire. "Just missed a tasty bite to eat."

The village had been a target for the dragon almost every day since it had taken up residence in the nearby mountains. Fortunately, help was at hand – from a very unlikely source.

Alberta the absent-minded witch happened to zoom over the mountains on her broomstick, just as the dragon was returning to its nest. Alberta, who always travelled too fast and who never looked where she was going, sailed right into the dragon's open mouth.

Now, to find yourself stuck in the foul-smelling mouth of a dragon would be enough to send even the nicest witch off the deep end. "Newts and toads!" she snapped, thinking the dragon had had the cheek to try to eat her. "You've bitten off a bit more than you can chew this time!"

Raising her magic wand, she cast a brilliant spell: *"A fearsome dragon you will not be. I'll wave this wand, just wait and see!"*

Then she conjured herself back to the comfort of her own home for a cup of slime tea.

Blissfully ignorant of the fact that a powerful spell had been cast upon it, the dragon returned to its nest.

"Dragon ahoy!" shouted the look-out the next day, as the dragon swooped down on the village once more. But the dreaded fiery jets of dragon breath never came, for when the enchanted dragon drew a deep breath and blew out with all its might, millions of sweet-smelling flower petals fluttered downwards from its gaping jaws.

Inside the castle, everyone started to laugh.

The dragon knew it was making a ridiculous spectacle of itself. No dragon worth its salt would blast a castle with flower petals! It flew away and never came back.

"Good riddance to you," the king called after the dragon.

Then everyone enjoyed a wonderful celebratory feast, before they lived happily ever after.

Hansel and Gretel

Hansel and Gretel lived by the forest with their father, a poor woodcutter, and their stepmother.

One evening, the family had nothing left to eat but a few crusts of bread. Hansel and Gretel went to bed hungry. As they lay in their beds, they heard the grown-ups talking.

"There are too many mouths to feed," said their stepmother. "We must take your children into the forest and leave them there."

"Never!" cried their father.

But the next morning, Hansel and Gretel's stepmother woke them early.

"Get up!" she ordered. "We're going into the forest to chop wood."

She handed them each a crust of bread for their lunch.

Hansel broke his bread into tiny pieces in his pocket, and as they walked, he secretly dropped a trail of crumbs on the ground.

Deep in the forest, Hansel and Gretel's father built them a fire.

"We are going to chop wood now," he said. "We'll return at sunset."

After a while, the children shared Gretel's bread, and then they curled up at the foot of an old oak tree and fell asleep.

When Hansel and Gretel woke up, they looked for the trail of breadcrumbs, but they were gone! The forest birds had eaten them.

"We'll wait till morning," Hansel said. "Then we can find our way home."

The next morning, the children walked through the forest, until they came to a little house – made of gingerbread! The roof was dripping with sugary icing, the door was made of candy canes and the garden was filled with colourful lollipops.

Delighted, the hungry children began to feast upon the sweets. As they ate, an old woman hobbled out of the house.

"You must be starving, my dears," she said. "Come inside and have a proper meal."

The old woman fed them well and then put them to bed.
But Hansel and Gretel didn't know that the kind old
woman was really a wicked witch. As she
watched them sleep, she cackled,
"I'll soon fatten these two
up. Then they will make a
proper meal for me!"

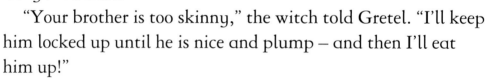

The following
morning, the witch
dragged Hansel from his
bed, and threw him into
a cage. Then she made
Gretel cook her brother
a big breakfast.

"Your brother is too skinny," the witch told Gretel. "I'll keep
him locked up until he is nice and plump – and then I'll eat
him up!"

Over the next few days, Hansel had as much food as he
could eat. And every morning, the witch made him stick out
his finger so she could feel whether he was fat enough to eat.

But Hansel knew that the old witch could hardly see, so he
stuck a chicken bone through the cage instead.

"Still too scrawny," the witch would say.

One day the witch got tired of waiting and decided to eat
Hansel right away.

"Light the oven!" the witch ordered Gretel. "Now crawl in
and see if it's hot enough."

Gretel knew the witch was planning to cook her as well. So she decided to trick the witch.

"The oven's much too small for me," she said.

"Nincompoop!" cried the witch. "Even I could get into that oven. Look!" And she stuck her head inside.

With a great big shove, Gretel pushed the witch into the oven and slammed the door shut.

Gretel freed Hansel from his cage, and they danced happily around the kitchen. "We're safe! We're safe!" they sang. When the children looked around the witch's house, they found chests crammed with gold and sparkling jewels. They filled their pockets and set off for home.

They seemed to find their way straight home, where their delighted father greeted them with hugs and kisses.

He told them that their cruel stepmother had died, so they had nothing to fear. Hansel and Gretel showed him the treasure they had found.

"We will never go hungry again!" they said. They all lived happily ever after.

Jade and the Jewels

Jade was the prettiest mermaid in the lagoon. Her jet-black hair reached right down to the tip of her swishy, fishy tail. Her eyes were as green as emeralds, and her skin was as white as the whitest pearl. And she knew it!

"That Jade thinks too much of herself!" the other mermaids would say. "One of these days she'll come unstuck."

Only one creature was fond of Jade. Gentle the giant turtle followed her wherever she went. But Jade didn't notice Gentle. She lived in her own world, spending all her time combing her hair and looking in the mirror.

One day Jade overheard the other mermaids talking about a pirate ship that had sunk to the bottom of the ocean. On board was a treasure chest filled with precious jewels. "But no one dares take the jewels," whispered the mermaids, "because the pirate ship is cursed!"

"I'm going to find that pirate ship," Jade thought. "Just imagine how beautiful I will look wearing all those jewels!" She set off right away.

Jade swam to a deep part of the ocean she had never been to before. She swam down and down until she found the shipwreck.

She saw the treasure chest through a porthole. Jade swam

inside and reached out to touch
the chest. The lid sprang open and
brilliant jewels spilled over the sides.

Jade lifted out a necklace and put it
round her neck. There was a little gold
and silver mirror in the chest. She held
it up to admire her reflection. It was
beautiful! Jade looked lovelier than
ever.

Suddenly, there was a loud crack
and the mirror shattered. The necklace turned to stone around
her neck – it was the ship's curse! Jade tried to swim, but the
necklace was so heavy she couldn't move.

"Help!" Jade cried out. "Help! Help!"

Gentle the giant turtle had followed Jade down to the
shipwreck. He heard her and swam to the porthole.

"Help me, Gentle," cried Jade, when she saw him. "Please
help me!"

Gentle's powerful flippers broke the necklace and freed Jade.
As they swam away from the wreck, Gentle said, "You don't
need fancy jewels, Jade. You're pretty without
them."

Once she was safely home, Jade
told the other mermaids that the
story about the curse was true.

"And I've learned my lesson," said
Jade. "I'll never be vain again."

How Butterflies Came to Be

One day, a long time ago, Elder Brother, the spirit of goodness, was out walking. The summer was over, the sky was blue, and everywhere he looked he saw the colours of autumn.

Soon Elder Brother arrived at a village where the women were grinding corn and children were playing happily together. He sat down feeling very content, as he enjoyed the beautiful autumn colours and the sound of birdsong.

Suddenly, Elder Brother became sad. "It will be winter soon," he thought. "The colourful autumn leaves will shrivel and fall, and the flowers will fade."

Elder Brother tried to think of a way to keep the autumn colours, so that everyone could enjoy them for longer.

Wherever he went, Elder Brother always carried a bag. Now he opened it up and started to fill it with the colours he saw all around him.

He took gold from a ray of sunlight and blue from the sky. He collected shiny black from a woman's hair and white from the cornmeal. He took green from the pine needles, red and yellow from the leaves, and purple and orange from the flowers.

When all the colours were in the bag, Elder Brother shook it. Then he thought of something else. He heard the birds singing and added their songs to the bag.

Elder Brother called the children over.
"**I have a surprise for you!**" he told them.
"Take this bag and open it."
The children opened the bag, and hundreds of colourful butterflies flew out. How the children laughed with joy! The women came over to see the butterflies too, and so did the men who had been working in the fields. Everyone stretched out their hands so the butterflies could land on them, and the butterflies started to sing as they fluttered around.

The people were delighted, but the birds were angry. One bird perched on Elder Brother's shoulder.

"Why have you given our songs to the butterflies?" the bird asked. "We were each given our own song and now you've given them away to creatures that have more beautiful colours than we do."

Elder Brother agreed and apologised to the birds. He took the songs away from the butterflies and gave them back to the birds. And that is how butterflies came to be — and why they are silent.

Sugarplum and the Butterfly

"Sugarplum," said the Fairy Queen, "I've got a very important job for you to do." Sugarplum was always given the most important work. The Fairy Queen said it was because she was the kindest and most helpful of all the fairies. "I want you to make a rose-petal ball gown for my birthday ball next week."

"It will be my pleasure," said Sugarplum happily.

Sugarplum began to gather cobwebs for the thread, and rose petals for the dress. While she was collecting the thread she found a butterfly caught in a cobweb.

"Oh, you poor thing," sighed Sugarplum.

Very carefully, she untangled the butterfly, but his wing was broken. Sugarplum laid the butterfly on a bed of feathers. She gathered some nectar from a special flower and fed him a drop at a time. Then she set about mending his wing with a magic spell.

After six days, the butterfly was better. He was very grateful. But now Sugarplum was behind with her work!

"Oh dear! I shall never finish the Fairy Queen's ball gown by tomorrow," she cried. "Whatever shall I do?"

The butterfly comforted her. "Don't worry, Sugarplum," he

said. "We'll help you."

He gathered all his friends together. There were yellow, blue, red and orange butterflies. He told them how Sugarplum had rescued him from the cobweb and helped to mend his wing.

The butterflies gladly gathered up lots of rose petals and dropped them next to Sugarplum. Then the butterflies flew away to gather more cobwebs, while Sugarplum arranged all the petals. Back and forth

went Sugarplum's hand with her needle and thread making the finest cobweb stitches. Sugarplum added satin ribbons and bows. When she had finished, Sugarplum was very pleased with the ball gown.

"Dear friend," she said to the butterfly, "I couldn't have finished the dress without your help."

"And I could never have flown again without your kindness and help," said the butterfly.

And the Fairy Queen was delighted with her new ball gown!

The Fox and the Stork

Once upon a time a fox decided to play a trick on his neighbour, the stork.

"Would you like to come and have supper with me?" he asked her one morning.

The stork was surprised by the invitation, because the fox had never been friendly to her before, but she happily accepted. He looked like a well-fed beast, and she was sure he would provide her with a good meal.

Every now and then, through the day, the stork caught the mouth-watering smell of the soup that the fox was preparing. By the time she arrived at his home she was feeling very hungry – which was exactly what the fox wanted.

"Enjoy your meal," said the crafty fox, ladling the soup into a shallow bowl. Of course, the fox was able to lap his up easily, but the stork could only dip the tip of her bill

into the soup. She wasn't able to drink a single drop!

"**Mmm, that was delicious,**" said the fox when he had slurped up the soup. "I see you don't have much of an appetite, so I will have yours, too."

The poor stork went home feeling hungrier than ever and was determined to take her revenge on the sly fox for playing such a mean trick. So the following week, she went to see him.

"Thank you for inviting me to supper last week," she said. "Now I would like to return the favour. Please come and dine with me this evening."

The fox was a little suspicious that the stork might want to get her own back, but he didn't see how she could possibly play a trick on him. After all, he was known for his cunning, and very few creatures had ever managed to outwit him.

All day long the fox looked forward to his supper, and by the evening he was very hungry. As he approached the stork's home he caught the appetising aroma of a fish stew and started to lick his lips.

But when the stork served the stew it was in a tall pot with a very narrow neck. The stork could reach the food easily with her long bill, but the fox could only lick the rim of the pot and sniff the tempting smell. Much as he didn't want to, the fox had to admit he had been outsmarted – and went home with an empty stomach!

Aesop's moral: One bad turn deserves another.

Six Swans

Once upon a time a king was tricked by an evil old witch into marrying her daughter. Now, the king had been married before, and had six sons and a beautiful daughter of his own, whom he loved very much. The king was afraid that the new queen would harm his children, so he hid them in a faraway castle. Even the king didn't know the way there. He had to roll a ball of magic string through the forest to show him the path.

The king secretly visited his children every evening. The new queen soon began to wonder where the king went each night. So she tricked one of the king's servants into telling her the secret. When she heard about the children, she knew she had to find them.

The very next day the queen searched the castle until she found the ball of magic string. Then, using a spell, she made some magic shirts of white silk.

When the king went hunting the next day, the queen took the magic ball of string and the shirts she had made and went to the hidden castle. As soon as the queen saw the six sons, she took out the magic shirts and quickly threw them over their heads. In a flash, they turned into swans and flew away.

When the sister returned home and
found her brothers gone, she went
in search of them. She wandered
for many days until she
came across a hunting
lodge. Inside were six
little beds. Suddenly,
the girl heard the
beating of wings, so
she hid beneath one of the
beds. Six white swans flew in through the window and landed
on the beds. The swans blew on one another and the girl
gasped with amazement. Their feathers fell off to reveal that
they weren't swans, but boys.

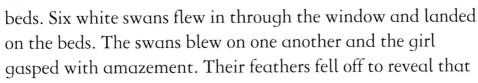

"My brothers!" she cried.

The boys were overjoyed to see their sister. But they were also
worried.

"You can't stay here," they said. "It's a robbers' den. If they
find you, they will be angry. Each day, we are human for just
fifteen minutes before we turn into swans again."

"How can I free you from the spell?" asked their sister.

"It is too much to ask. You must sew six shirts from nettles," said
one brother. "And you must not utter a word for six years."

"I will do it," cried the sister.

And with that, her brothers turned back into swans again.

The princess went out and began picking nettles at once.

She did not mind that they stung her soft fingers. She simply sat under a tree and began to sew.

Before long, a king from another kingdom rode by.

"What are you doing?" he asked.

Of course, the girl could not speak. She just kept on sewing, trying not to flinch as the nettles stung her hands.

The king fell in love on the spot. He took the girl home and married her. But still the girl would not speak, and every day she insisted on sewing her nettle shirts.

The king's mother was jealous of the new queen and wanted to get rid of her. When the girl had her first baby, the king's mother stole the child and gave it to a woodcutter. She told everyone the queen had given the baby away.

Of course, the queen would not speak to defend herself. She just kept on sewing. Luckily, the king did not believe his mother.

A year later, the queen had another baby, and once again the king's mother gave the child to the woodcutter.

"Now do you believe me?" she asked of the king.

The king shook his head.

But when their third child disappeared, the king began to have doubts.

"She only wants to sew all day," he thought. "Maybe Mother speaks the truth."

The king begged his wife to defend herself, but she would not. Sadly, the king decided she was guilty.

"You will be punished in the morning," he announced.

The queen sewed all night. It was the last night of the six years she had been given to complete the nettle shirts.

At sunrise, the six shirts were almost finished. Only one sleeve was missing. When the king came for the queen, the six white swans appeared out of thin air. The queen threw the nettle shirts over their heads. At once, the swans turned into boys – though the youngest had a wing instead of an arm.

"At last I can speak," cried the girl. She quickly told the king about her brothers, and how his own mother had given their children to the woodcutter.

When the king heard the truth, he sent his mother away and went to rescue his children, from the woodcutter.

After that, the king, queen, their children and the six brothers lived happily ever after.